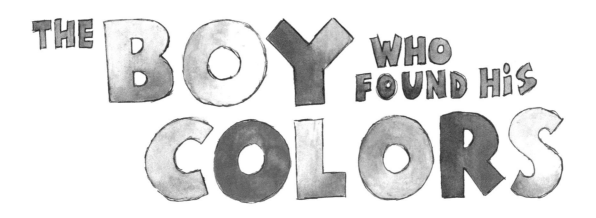

THE BOY WHO FOUND HIS COLORS

WRITTEN AND ILLUSTRATED BY ALYSSA RAE MEYER

For you, Blue.

Published by Orange Hat Publishing 2018
ISBN 978-1-948365-67-3

Copyrighted © 2018 by Alyssa Meyer
All Rights Reserved
The Boy Who Found His Colors
Written and illustrated by Alyssa Meyer

www.orangehatpublishing.com

THE BOY WHO FOUND HIS COLORS

WRITTEN AND ILLUSTRATED BY ALYSSA RAE MEYER

Once there was a town on top of a hill all covered in black and grey,
and in this town the villagers would go along their same old ways.
Every day they'd walk, heads down, not daring to smile or speak.
They all walked quickly from place to place every day of the week.

Now in this town there was a boy
who was different from the rest.
He dreamt of colors – blues and greens
and oranges he liked the best.

One day he asked his mom,
"Mother, can I paint some colors around?"

His mom gasped and scolded him,
"Dear me! No! Not ever in this town!"

"Go to bed," she said,
"without any dinner.
And never ask about colors again.
We are perfectly happy with the way things are,
and don't ask what, why, or when."

But the boy knew he could not be happy
in this town of grey and black,
so he quietly snuck out the front door
with nothing but his rucksack.

He walked through the streets of the black and grey town
and journeyed all through the night,
and just when the sun came over the hills,
he gasped at a most wondrous sight.

The boy looked up at towering buildings of the most colorful town he'd seen.
Yellow bricks and blue skies and trees in rows of green.
There were houses of rubies, roads of gold, and even birds of pink,
and the people in this colorful town looked at him with a smile and a wink.

"Hello," beamed a short, plump man
with a mustache as gold as his watch.
"Nice to meet you.
I am the Mayor, Mr. Butterscotch.
How do you do, my fine young lad?
What brings you to this town?"

The boy looked up at the short, round man
and said with a little frown,
"I come from a place far away
where colors aren't meant to be seen.
It makes me sad to live in a world
where grey is so routine."

Mr. Butterscotch put a gentle arm around the boy and said,
"No worries, lad, in this happy place you can find all sorts of friends!"

They walked down
rows and rows of buildings
all towering in yellows and greens
and stopped to smell
the red daffodils
and marveled at
lines of blue jeans.

The boy looked down and gasped to see
his shirt had turned red and gold.
His pants were green,
his bag turned pink,
and his shoes became a bright rainbow.

"My boy! You are a wonderful sight!
How do your colors feel?"

The boy beamed up at the Mayor and said,
"I feel so very real!"

The boy spent weeks and weeks in this town
doing whatever he liked,
and he felt completely happy and calm
for the first time in his life.

As time passed, however,
he started to feel
guilty and sad in his head,
and he started to miss
his routine family
and even his
black and grey bed.

"Mr. Mayor," he said,
"I think I must go back home to my family,
but I'm scared to leave all these colors behind
and go back to being the old me."

The Mayor laughed
and shook his head saying,
"My boy, you've gone astray!
These colors are a part of you
that no one can take away.
Go home to your family
and your friends
in that little black and grey town,
but never lose the colors you've found,
and don't let people drag you down."

So the boy grabbed his little rucksack
and skipped on through the day
until he came upon the familiar sight
of his town all covered in grey.

"My son!" cried his father.
"Where have you been?
We were scared you wouldn't return."

His mother saw his new bright clothes
and shook her head with concern.

But the boy looked calmly at his mom and said,
"Mother, this is me,
and if you can't love me for the colors I wear,
then I cannot fully be free."

"My dear," she cried, "you are so brave
for showing your colorful self.
I wish I could be more like you
in showing my truest self."

The boy reached into his tiny rucksack
and pulled out a scarf of blue.
"Here you go, Mother.
You can take my scarf
and make it a part of you."

So the boy and his parents went out on the town that once was all covered in grey
and shared all his colors with everyone for the rest of the day.
From then on out the town was changed and the boy was never alone,
because he found colors within himself and made them all his own.

Alyssa is a creative storyteller from the Midwest. Her passions include crafting poetic stories and creating art with her favorite mediums of watercolor, ink, and charcoal. She is inspired by emotional expression, the natural world, and individuality. This is her first story.

CPSIA information can be obtained
at www.ICGtesting.com
Printed in the USA
BVHW022118140422
634159BV00005B/7